Rookie español   P9-BJY-079

CARLITOS FRIOLENTO

**Escrito por
Dana Meachen Rau**

**Ilustrado por
Martin Lemelman**

Children's Press®
Una división de Scholastic Inc.
Nueva York • Toronto • Londres • Auckland • Sydney
Ciudad de México • Nueva Delhi • Hong Kong
Danbury, Connecticut

PARA EL VERDADERO CARLITOS
—D. M. R.

PARA SAM
—M. L.

Especialista de la lectura
Katharine A. Kane
Especialista de la educación
(Jubilada de la Oficina de Educación del Condado de San Diego,
California y de la Universidad Estatal de San Diego)

Traductora
Jacqueline M. Córdova, Ph.D.
Universidad Estatal de California, Fullerton

Visite a Children's Press® en el Internet a:
http://publishing.grolier.com

Información de publicación de la Biblioteca del Congreso de los EE.UU.
Rau, Dana Meachen.
   [Chilly Charlie. Spanish]
   Carlitos friolento / escrito por Dana Meachen Rau ; ilustrado por Martin
Lemelman.
      p. cm. — (Rookie español)
   Resumen: Carlitos siente frío por todo el cuerpo y necesita que alguien le
de un abrazo para abrigarle.
   ISBN 0-516-22352-6 (lib. bdg.)   0-516-26208-4 (pbk.)
   [1. Frío—ficción. 2. Abrazos—ficción. 3. Cuentos rimados. 4. Libros en español.]
I. Lemelman, Martin, il. II. Título. III. Serie.
PZ74.3 .R335 2001
[E]—dc21

                        00-065714

©2001 Dana Meachen Rau
Ilustraciones ©2001 Martin Lemelman
Todos los derechos reservados. Publicado simultáneamente en Canadá.
Impreso en los Estados Unidos de América.
1 2 3 4 5 6 7 8 9 10 R 10 09 08 07 06 05 04 03 02 01

GROLIER
PUBLISHING

Carlitos siempre
siente frío

en los dedos de las manos,

y en los dedos de los pies.

Siente frío en los codos,

en las mejillas

y en la nariz.

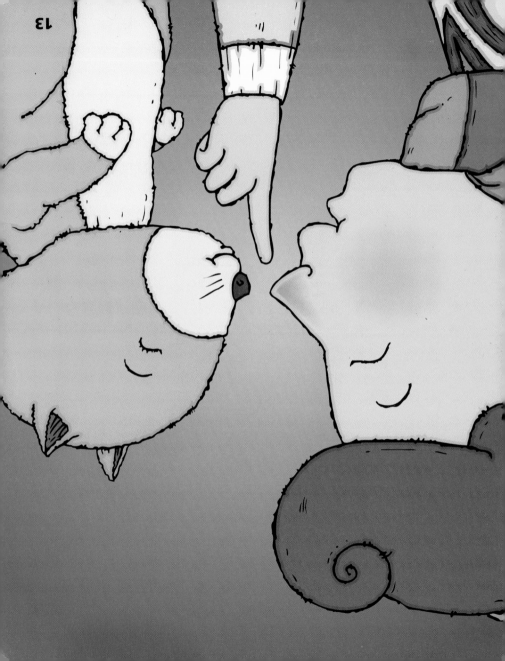

¿Cómo puede abrigarse Carlitos?

¿Con una taza de chocolate calientito?

¿Cobijarle, bien envueltito?

¡No!

¡Carlitos necesita estar bien abrazadito!

Lista de palabras (32 palabras)

abrazadito	dedos	nariz
abrigarse	en	necesita
bien	envueltito	no
calientito	estar	pies
Carlitos	frío	puede
cobijarle	friolento	siempre
codos	la	siente
cómo	las	taza
con	los	una
chocolate	manos	y
de	mejillas	

Sobre la autora

Dana Meachen Rau ha escrito muchos libros para niños, incluyendo libros de ficción histórica, cuentos, biografías y varios libros de la serie Rookie Reader. También trabaja como ilustradora y redactora. Cuando no se encuentra ni utilizando la computadora para escribir ni buscando algún papelito desviado, toma chocolate con su esposo Chris y su hijo Carlitos en Farmington, Connecticut.

Sobre el ilustrador

Martin Lemelman está muy ocupado, viviendo su segunda niñez en Allentown, Pennsylvania, con su esposa Monica y sus cuatro hijos, todos los cuales son críticos del arte. Ha creado ilustraciones para muchas revistas y libros para niños. También es profesor del Departamento de Diseño en la Comunicación de la Universidad de Kutztown. Este libro es el primero en que colabora para Children's Press.

SO-AAD-483

The  Pebble First Guide to

Songbirds

by Katy R. Kudela

Consulting Editor: Gail Saunders-Smith, PhD

Consultant: Laura Erickson, Science Editor
Cornell Laboratory of Ornithology
Ithaca, New York

Capstone
press®

Mankato, Minnesota

Pebble Books are published by Capstone Press,
1710 Roe Crest Drive, North Mankato, Minnesota 56003.
www.capstonepub.com

Copyright © 2009 by Capstone Press, a Capstone imprint.
All rights reserved. No part of this publication may be reproduced in whole
or in part, or stored in a retrieval system, or transmitted in any form or by any
means, electronic, mechanical, photocopying, recording, or otherwise,
without written permission of the publisher.
For information regarding permission, write to Capstone Press,
1710 Roe Crest Drive, North Mankato, Minnesota 56003.
Printed in the United States of America in North Mankato, Minnesota.
032012
006661R

Library of Congress Cataloging-in-Publication Data
Kudela, Katy R.
    The pebble first guide to songbirds / by Katy R. Kudela.
    p. cm. — (Pebble books. Pebble first guides)
    Includes bibliographical references and index.
    Summary: "A basic field guide format introduces 13 songbirds. Includes color
photographs and range maps" — Provided by publisher.
    ISBN-13: 978-1-4296-2244-8 (hardcover)   ISBN-10: 1-4296-2244-X (hardcover)
    ISBN-13: 978-1-4296-3442-7 (paperback)   ISBN-10: 1-4296-3442-1 (paperback)
    1. Songbirds — Juvenile literature. I. Title. II. Series.
QL696.P2K83 2009
598.8 — dc22   2008028237

About Songbirds

A songbird is a bird with special feet for perching on branches.
Songbirds also have a special voice box to communicate with
calls and songs. For most kinds of songbirds, only the males
sing. Songs warn other males to stay away. Songs also help
male songbirds find a mate.

Note to Parents and Teachers

The Pebble First Guides set supports science standards related to life science.
In a reference format, this book describes and illustrates 13 songbirds. This
book introduces early readers to subject-specific vocabulary words, which
are defined in the Glossary section. Early readers may need assistance to
read some words and to use the Table of Contents, Glossary, Read More,
Internet Sites, and Index sections of the book.

Table of Contents

Height:	16 to 21 inches (41 to 53 centimeters)
Wingspan:	33 to 39 inches (84 to 99 centimeters)
Eats:	insects, seeds, grains, fruit, garbage
Lives:	open areas with a few trees
Facts:	• stores food in hiding places
	• mates for life

4

American Crow Range

☐ North America

young crows

American Goldfinch

male

female

Height:	4 to 5 inches (10 to 13 centimeters)
Wingspan:	7 to 9 inches (18 to 23 centimeters)
Eats:	seeds
Lives:	weedy fields, orchards, gardens
Facts:	• builds nest with thistle seeds • sometimes called the wild canary

American Goldfinch Range

☐ North America

young

American Robin

eggs

Height:	8 to 11 inches (20 to 28 centimeters)
Wingspan:	12 to 16 inches (30 to 41 centimeters)
Eats:	earthworms, insects, fruit
Lives:	forests, woodlands, gardens
Facts:	• young robins have spotted breasts • easily sees earthworms in their holes

American Robin Range

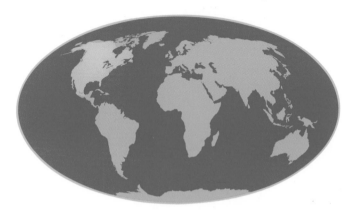

☐ North America

adult with chicks

Baltimore Oriole

Height:	7 to 8 inches (18 to 20 centimeters)
Wingspan:	9 to 12 inches (23 to 30 centimeters)
Eats:	caterpillars, fruit, insects, nectar
Lives:	open areas with a few tall trees
Facts:	• nest hangs from outer tree branches • also called the golden robin

Baltimore Oriole Range

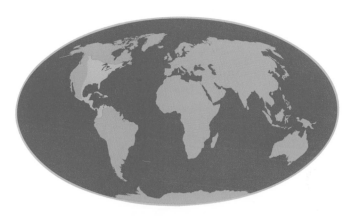

□ North America, Central America, South America

female

male

nest

Black-capped Chickadee

Height:	5 to 6 inches (13 to 15 centimeters)
Wingspan:	6 to 8 inches (15 to 20 centimeters)
Eats:	insects, seeds, berries
Lives:	forests, open areas with large trees
Facts:	• remembers thousands of places where it hides food
	• can survive freezing cold winters

Black-capped Chickadee Range

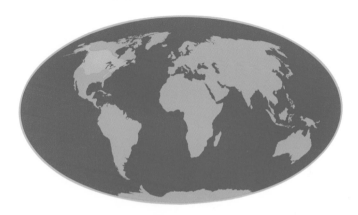

☐ North America

chicks

Blue Jay

Height:	10 to 12 inches (25 to 30 centimeters)
Wingspan:	13 to 17 inches (33 to 43 centimeters)
Eats:	insects, nuts, fruit, seeds
Lives:	oak trees
Facts:	• screeches like a hawk
	• mates for life

14

Blue Jay Range

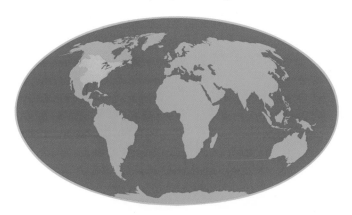

☐ North America

adult with young

15

Eastern Bluebird

male

female

Height:	6 to 8 inches (15 to 20 centimeters)
Wingspan:	10 to 13 inches (25 to 33 centimeters)
Eats:	insects, small fruit
Lives:	orchards, parks, pastures
Facts:	• nests in holes in trees
	• some nest in birdhouses

Eastern Bluebird Range

☐ North America, Central America

eggs

adult with young

House Finch

female · male

Height:	5 to 6 inches (13 to 15 centimeters)
Wingspan:	8 to 10 inches (20 to 25 centimeters)
Eats:	buds, seeds, fruit
Lives:	spruce trees, oak trees, grasslands
Facts:	• colors in food make males' feathers yellow or red • build nests in hanging plant baskets

18

House Finch Range

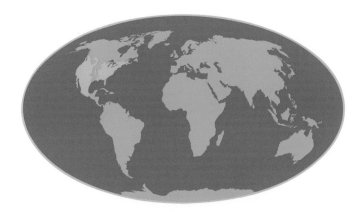

☐ North America

adults with chicks

Indigo Bunting

male

Height:	5 to 5.5 inches (13 to 14 centimeters)
Wingspan:	7 to 9 inches (18 to 23 centimeters)
Eats:	insects, spiders, seeds, buds, berries
Lives:	hedgerows, fruit trees, weedy fields
Facts:	• adult males look brown in fall and winter
	• migrates at night and follows the stars

Indigo Bunting Range

☐ North America, Central America, South America

female with chicks

female

male

Height:	8 to 9 inches (20 to 23 centimeters)
Wingspan:	10 to 12 inches (25 to 30 centimeters)
Eats:	seeds, fruit, buds, insects
Lives:	shrubs, small trees
Facts:	• both males and females sing
	• state bird of seven U.S. states

Northern Cardinal Range

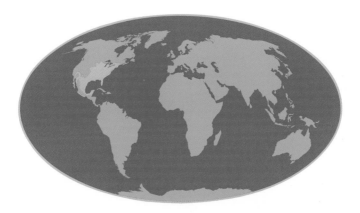

☐ North America, Central America

female with chicks

23

Northern Mockingbird

Height:	8 to 10 inches (20 to 25 centimeters)
Wingspan:	12 to 14 inches (30 to 36 centimeters)
Eats:	fruit, insects
Lives:	thickets, desert brush, shrubs
Facts:	• males copy new songs and sounds • females do not sing much

Northern Mockingbird Range

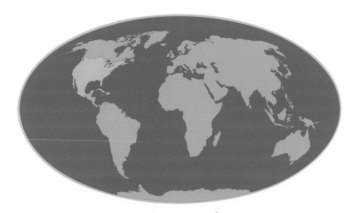

□ North America, Caribbean islands

adult with chicks

25

Red-winged Blackbird

male

Height:	7 to 9 inches (18 to 23 centimeters)
Wingspan:	12 to 16 inches (30 to 41 centimeters)
Eats:	insects, seeds, grains
Lives:	marshes, meadows, alfalfa fields
Facts:	• named for red patches on adult male
	• often builds nest near water

Red-winged Blackbird Range

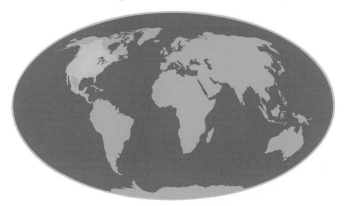

☐ North America, Central America

female with chicks

White-breasted Nuthatch

Height:	5 to 6 inches (13 to 15 centimeters)
Wingspan:	8 to 11 inches (20 to 28 centimeters)
Eats:	insects, nuts, seeds
Lives:	maple trees, birch trees, oak trees
Facts:	• climbs down tree trunks headfirst
	• flies with chickadee flocks in winter